This book belongs to

Children's
POOLBEG

First published 1989 by
Poolbeg Press Ltd.
Knocksedan House,
Swords, Co. Dublin, Ireland.

© Eamon Kelly 1989

This book is published with the assistance of
The Arts Council/An Chomhairle Ealaíon, Ireland.

ISBN 1 85371 053 9

Cover design by Pomphrey Associates
Typeset by Print-Forme,
62 Santry Close, Dublin 9.
Printed by The Guernsey Press Ltd.,
Vale, Guernsey, Channel Islands.

The Bridge of Feathers

The Bridge of Feathers
Eamon Kelly

Children's
POOLBEG

Contents

The Bridge of Feathers

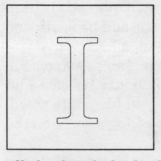t happened one time that there was a king living in Ireland, and all the family he had was one only son. A fine boy he was too, and the king was very fond of him.

This day the king's son was playing ball in the big field in front of his father's mansion, when who should he see coming towards him but an old grey man riding on a white steed. He rode up to where the young lad was and he asked the king's son would he like to play the ball with him. The king's son said he didn't care ... he would. The two began to play and the king's son won the game.

"Well now," says the old grey man, "I'll be here again to-morrow evening and let you be here too."

"All right," says the king's son. "I will."

And he went home and told the king what transpired, and the king was very down and out when he heard it.

"That man," says the king, "is Old Grey Norris, and as long as you'll play with him, and you'll have to now, in the end he'll win and you'll have to do what he says."

The following evening the king's son was in the field kicking the ball when he saw Old Grey Norris coming riding on his white steed. They began to play and the king's son won the second game.

"Your luck won't always hold, Garsún," says Old Grey Norris, "I'll be here again to-morrow evening."

Which he was on the dot. The game began, and at the beginning the king's son had all the play, but the tide turned and nothing would go right for him and Old Grey Norris won the game.

"You'll have to come away with me now," says he to the king's son. And he had to go, there was no way out of it. The king's son sat up behind Old Grey Norris on the white steed, and they travelled all through the night and all through the following day, and coming up to nightfall they came at long last to Old Grey Norris's place. The king's son was given his supper, and Old Grey Norris told him to be off to bed now and that he'd call him early in the morning. He did, and he brought the king's son out to a hayfield and he said:

"My grandmother lost a darning needle in this field about twenty years ago. You have the whole day to try for it, and if you don't find it before night I'll take your sacred life ... bainfear an ceann díot."

The king's son got a fierce fright when he said that. And he gave the whole day trying for the needle, going on his hands and knees over every square inch of the field, and it failed him. He never found it. So when the sun was sinking he sat down, putting his head in his hand and saying: "What will I do now." He was not long there at all when someone tapped him on the shoulder and looking up there was the grandest young girl he ever saw in his life standing alongside him. "Why," says she "are you so upset?".

"I'm upset," says he, "because I can't find the needle."

"Well now," says she, "I'll find that needle for you in no time, but don't tell my father." Old Grey Norris was married by all accounts and this was his daughter. "Don't mention my name," she said, "if you do it is as much as my life is worth."

And she walked from him over to the headland and she pulled up a plant—'twas like a buachalán* or something—and she shook it and the needle fell out of the roots— wouldn't he have a job to find it! "Seo," says she, "tóg é, ach na tabhair do'n sean-duine é.# Keep it yourself, it might come in handy to you yet."

She went away with herself and she wasn't gone when Old Grey Norris came, and he said to the king's son:

"Did you find the darning needle?"

"I did," he said.

"Show it to me," says he.

"I'll show it to you," he said, "but I won't give it to you. I'm keeping it myself."

And he put the darning needle in the lapel of his coat. I'd say myself that Old Grey Norris was wondering how he found the needle, but he didn't say anything only:

"Go on in to your supper and clear off to bed, I'll call you again early in the morning."

He had the king's son out off the bed at cockcrow in the morning and bringing him to the bank of a river Old Grey Norris said: "I've

* Rag-weed
# "take it, but do not give it to the old man."

a very hard job for you now, I want you to make a bridge of feathers to span that river."

He gave him a shotgun and told him to shoot wild fowl and with their feathers to make the bridge. "And if you haven't it made by nightfall," he said, "remember what I said yesterday, bainfear an ceann díot!"*

The king's son shot a pile of birds and plucked them until he had a mountain of feathers and then he began to build the bridge and you would never believe how hard that job is until you would go about it. And to make things worse the day turned windy and the feathers began to rise—the air was full of them like snowflakes and here was the king's son trying to retrieve them and to keep 'em down and hold them in position. In between the squalls of wind he was able to make some shape at building the piers but if the cat went a pound he could not turn the arch, so he had to throw his head with it, for it could not be done. And when the sun was sinking he sat down for he was very go brónach.# With that someone tapped him on the shoulder. He looked up agus cé bheadh ann ach an bhean dubh álainnø—

---

* The head will be cut off you
# sorrowful
ø and who should be there but the dark young lady.

Old Grey Norris's black haired daughter.

"Why are you so downhearted," she said. "I'm downhearted," says he, "because I can't make the bridge of feathers."

"Walk on down there for a bit," she said. He did, and she set to work making the bridge and when 'twas finished there was nothing ever seen like it within the four walls of the world. It was a pure marvel, from pier to arch and arch to parapet! And you'd hardly think it was real, but it was for they linked arms and walked across it. Look at that! They walked a while and then she went to her father's house.

After a piece Old Grey Norris came and he asked the king's son did he make the bridge. "The bridge is made," the king's son said. "Come on away," says he, "until we see it." And when he saw the bridge his eyes widened in wonder.

"You never made that bridge," he said, "but whether you did or not, you'll not be able for the job I'll give you to-morrow."

That night after his supper the girl came to the king's son and told him to clear out of this place.

"As long as you stay here," she said, "Old Grey Norris will get the upper hand of you. Tomorrow he's planning to send you to the

Valley of Fire for the three burned sparks.
There's a black horse in the stable, take him
and I'll go with you to show you the way."

When darkness fell the king's son saddled
the black horse, put the girl sitting behind him
and galloped for home. They travelled all
through the night and when the sun was rising
in the heavens, the girl said: "Look behind you
and see do you see anything."

"There's a black speck on the horizon," he
said.

They galloped on and in a while's time the
girl said: "Look behind you and see do you see
anything." He looked back and there was the
white steed.

"'Tis Old Grey Norris," he said.

"Quick," says she, "the darning needle.
Throw it back over you shoulder."

He did and a wall of spikes shot up from the
ground and no living thing could go through it.
They kept going and when the sun was high in
the heavens the girl said to the young lad:

"Look behind and see do you see anything."
"There's another black speck on the horizon,"
he said. They were going like the wind now
and after a time the girl said to the king's son:

"Look behind you and see do you see
anything."

"Oh glory," say he, " 'tis Old Grey Norris and he's getting closer every minute."

He gave the spur to the horse now and as quick as they were going 'twasn't long till they heard the pounding of the hooves behind 'em. The girl said then to the king's son:

"Put your hand in the horse's ear and see is there a drop of sweat there."

"There is," he said.

"Throw it back over your shoulder," she said. He threw the drop of sweat behind him and a big lake sprang up from the ground. They went by the stepping stones and he went by the ford. They were saved and Old Grey Norris was drowned and indeed there was no one crying after him.

The king's son went on to his father's house and he said to the king:

"Do you know this girl?"

"I don't," says the king.

"Why then," says he, "she saved my life," telling him the whole story, "and I'm planning to marry her now.

And they were married the following week and everyone that was anyone was at the wedding, so put a sod on the fire, give an apple to the child and pour a drink for the storyteller.

The House Under the Sea

I remember one time I was talking to a man from the seaside, and he told me he was one day down by the strand and he came across a young seal, and he caught him and put him a bag and brought him home and threw him under the table.

There was a crowd of the neighbours in that night playing cards, and around ten o'clock they heard someone below on the strand and he calling:

"Timmie. Where are you, Timmie?"

They went out and down to the strand thinking maybe that there was some boatmen in trouble, but when they went down they couldn't see anyone. It was a fine bright moonlight night. They doubled back to the house and they were no sooner inside than they heard the call again:

"Timmie. Where are you, Timmie?"

Well, they couldn't make hog, dog nor devil of it. It wasn't the voice of anyone they knew. They opened the door wide and the call came nearer:

"Timmie. Do you hear me, Timmie? Why don't you come out to me?"

They looked from one to the other, changing colour, and one man said:

"Who's Timmie?"

"I'm Timmie," says the seal under the table, "and that's my brother Johnny calling me!"

I tell you they weren't long lifting up the bag, opening the mouth of it, putting it outside the door and saying:

"Well if you're Timmie, off with you to Johnny. And don't be putting the heart crossways in us!"

"Would you believe that!" says the man from the seaside.

"Why wouldn't I believe it," says I, "when I had a far more remarkable experience myself." And I told him the story exactly as I am going to tell it to you now.

I am a stone mason by trade, I began, and it was the time we were building the pier in Ballinskelligs, and I was this day walking down by the sea when a man came along in a boat.

"Will you come for a drive," says he.

"I will," says I.

"Get in," says he.

And I did. He had a gun in the bottom of the boat and when we were gone awhile we saw something black bobbing in the water. "A seal," says he, taking aim and as he fired the seal ducked.We pulled over to the place and wasn't there a pool of blood on top of the waves.

"Ah ha," says he, "I knew I hit him. "We'll hold on here now for a while and that seal will float up on the tide to us."

We threw out the anchor and waited, but if we were there yet the seal wouldn't float. The sea was turning rough, the horses shaking their white manes, and it looked like as if we were in for squalls, so we said we would move on. The man went to pull the anchor but if the cat went a pound he couldn't knock a shake out of it.

"Play tough," says I, "and I'll go down to see what's holding it." A very foolish remark too, now that I come to think of it!

"Be cautious!" says he.

And I came out of the coat and handed him my hat, took a deep breath and down with me, and I thought I'd never come to the end of the chain it was so long. With that, my toe struck something solid. I looked down and where was the hook of the anchor, curled in under the lintel of a door! I hopped off on the ground and where was I? Standing in front of a long, low, thatched, whitewashed house.

"Come on away in," says someone talking inside.

I straightened my tie and faced in and the man of the house got up to welcome me, and I noticed that he was wearing a bandage around his head.

"Is it anyone hit you," says I, all concern.

"You should know that," says he, "or that specimen that was in the boat with you. Only for I ducking so quick he'd have left the daylight into my brains! And isn't it a fright," says he, "that a man can't put his nose out for a puff of air without someone having a cork at him, or is there any law or order in the world above?"

"Well now," says I, "I'm not a shooting man myself."

"Nor you haven't the cut of it," he said. "I've only to look at you, you wouldn't hurt a fly. Take a chair and sit down. You must be starved with the hunger."

And 'twas true for him. A spell in the salt air and you would chew ivy after it. His wife a small, compact, little woman was there too, very busy over the fire.

"Close out the door one of ye," says she, "the wind is turning the smoke on me."

The door was banged out, sweeping the anchor before it. Up it flew and there was I cut off from the world above. A nice predicament to be in!

"Don't you fret," says the man of the house. "You can stay the night with us. We'll fix up a shakedown, some place for you! Woman," says he then calling the wife, "take up the eggs or we'll have to get hammers to 'em."

The table was laid for the supper so we all sat over, the man and his wife, his four sons and his three daughters, and talk of hospitality, they did not know what to make of me. "Shove up the bread to the man … pass down the milk … will you have another egg … don't be sparing 'em … eat your fill … and let tomorrow take care of itself." Such nice people, and so freemaking! You'd cover a lot of ground to-day before you would meet their likes.

And not like here they wouldn't be one minute idle. No sooner was the table cleared and the ware washed than the mother and the daughters were carding and spinning wool, and the sons were drawing in sheafs of oats and scotching them on the backs of chairs, and the old man, sore and all as the head was by him, turned in to pointing scolbs* and 'twas plain that they would be putting a new coat of thatch on the house in the morning, which they were first thing after the breakfast.

I knocked out in the yard. It was in the settle bed near the fire I spend the night. Oh, it was so comfortable, it was like a wren's nest. I knocked out in the yard as I said, and after throwing my eye along the roof I said to the man of the house.

"Blessed hour tonight, what happened your chimney stack?"

"Well," says he, "like everyone else around here, 'tis a wickerwork one I had, made of rods, and I pulled it down for 'twas rotten."

"Well now," says I, "if you can get the loan of a mason's traps you have a man standing here on the sod that'll have a stone chimney stack up for you while you'd be winking."

"I hear," says he, "They're the coming thing."

"If you had an air to that," says I, "You could

* split and pointed rods for thatching

sing it."

So he went away and he got a trowel,
hammer and plumb rule. He drew stones, got
lime and sand and made mortar, and I fell into
work and in no time at all I had the new
chimney stack built, with a nice projecting
ledge and a saw-toothed slate all round the
flue to keep the jackdaws from perching on it,
for no word of a lie they can be an awful
nuisance. I looked down then and the yard
was full of seal people all very taken by the
new chimney stack, and every man of them
wanting one of the self same pattern on top of
his own house. So I went away building
chimney stacks till I lost all track of time.

Then one morning I said to the man of the
house.

"I wonder will I ever again see the world
above?"

"What a hurry you're in," says he, "are you
getting tired of us?"

"Ah 'tisn't that at all," I said, "but they'll be
wondering where I am at home."

"Well in that case," says he, "you can go to-
day. Woman," he called to his wife, "where is
my overcoat?"

She brought it and he put it on, and he
looked like a seal now. I hopped up on his back

and he made one spring and shot up through the waves and in two shakes he had me in above at Cuas a 'Mhadra Uisge. I thanked him, and looked around and there wasn't a sinner in view. I moved up on the high ground and I saw all the cars above around the chapel.

" 'Tis Sunday," says I "and the people are inside at Mass."

I ran up and I was just into the porch in time to hear myself being prayed for from the altar!

Creid é no ná creid tá sé sin fíor!*

* Believe it or not that is true!

The Wheelwright's Son

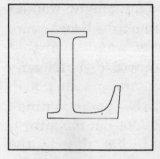ong ago in Ireland there was this man and by trade he was a wheelwright, and he worked every day in his workshop making wheels and his young son helped him. Now, not far away there lived a powerful landlord that owned all the land and the poor people had to pay him big rent for the small houses in which they lived.

That landlord had a little daughter and this night she dreamt she would one day wash the feet of the wheelwright's son in a golden basin. There was a basin like that in the landlord's house but it was only the size of a sugar bowl. She had the same dream the second night, and again the third night about washing the feet of the wheelwright's son in the little golden basin.

When she woke the third morning she

brought the little golden basin to her father and told him about the dream she had. "And how will I wash his feet," says she, "in a little basin as small as that?"

The landlord, by the way, made no wonder of the dream, but at the same time he was very troubled in case the dream was a sign that later on in life his daughter would get friendly with the wheelwright's son and maybe marry him. This was something the landlord didn't want to happen, and to make double sure it wouldn't happen he went that day to the wheelwright and said he, the wheelwright, would have to send his son away out of the province and put him to a new trade.

"He is the only child we have," the wheelwright and his wife said, "and what would we do without him?"

"If you don't do what I say," says the landlord, "I have the power to put you out of your house and you will have no place to earn a living."

A landlord's word was law at that time and the wheelwright had to give in. Next morning he walked away with his son to put him to a new trade, and when they were walking for three days they met a tall man in black clothes. And he said to the wheelwright:

"Where are you going with your son?"

And the wheelwright said: "To the province of Leinster to find him a new trade."

"Well now," says the Man in the Black Clothes, "if you let him come with me for the space of a year I'll teach him a fine trade."

"Maith mar a thárla,"* says the wheelwright, "but be sure to bring my son back safe and sound when the year is up."

The Man in the Black Clothes said he would, and the wheelwright came home and for him and his wife that was a long year looking forward every day to the time when their son would walk in the door to them again.

When the year was up there was a knock at the door and who was there but the Man in the Black Clothes, and the wheelwright's son. His father and mother hardly knew their son he got so big and so handsome. There was no doubt about it but he seemed to be well fed and well cared for.

"How is he getting on at his trade?" says the wheelwright.

"Well now," says the Man in the Black Clothes, "he'd want a little more time before he'll be able to show the results of my

* Well and good.

training."

"Alright," says the wheelwright, "but on one condition that you bring him back safe and sound to me at the end of that time."

The Man in the Black Clothes said he would and they went away and when the second year was up there was a knock at the door and in walked the Man in the Black Clothes, and the wheelwright's son. If anything the son looked finer and more handsome than the year before.

They sat down and they were talking and the wheelwright said:

"How is my son getting on at his trade?"

"Hop out there," says the Man in the Black Clothes to the son, "and show your father and mother what you have learned."

The son walked out into the middle of the kitchen, jumped the height of himself off the ground, and changed himself into a fox and ran out the door. The father and mother were speechless when they saw that. In a while's time they heard a lot of clitter in the yard and in came the son in his own shape driving a field full of geese before him.

"Take those geese away," says the wheelwright, "I don't want the whole parish coming here to the door in the morning looking for their geese. I am no robber!"

"Don't be afraid," says the Man in the Black Clothes, "no one will ever come demanding those geese, for those geese never belonged to anyone. You see now the fine trade your son is learning!"

"Whatever trade it is I don't like it," says the wheelwright.

"Let him come with me for another year," says the Man in the Black Clothes, "and there'll be no magician in Europe to touch him."

"Do what he says," says the son, "just for one year more."

"Alright so," says the wheelwright.

They went away, and when they were gone 'twas then the wheelwright thought of it. He never said to the Man in the Black Clothes to bring back his son when the year would be up.

"Oh what were you thinking about," says his wife, "that you didn't remember that. We'll never see him again now."

And sure enough when the year was up the son did not come. The father waited one month and two months and three months, but there was no sign of his son.

Then one fine morning the wheelwright put on his new clothes, polished his shoes, and said to his wife:

"I'm going away now and I won't sit the second time to the same table, or sleep the second night in the same bed till I find my son."

And he went away and he was walking for three days and three weeks and three years, but nowhere did he hear any word about his son.

Then one morning he met a medium built, well preserved, fat, bulky little man with a red beard.

"I know your trouble," says the small man, "and come on away with me and while we're walking I'll tell you where to find your son and I'll tell you how you'll know your son and the way you'll know him is, one pigeon will have a crooked feather in his tail. What did I say?"

"You said," says the wheelwright, "that one pigeon will have a crooked feather in his tail."

"You have your lesson off," says the small man. "Do you see that mansion! Go up there now and remember what I said."

The wheelwright went up to the mansion and who opened the door and came out but the Man in the Black Clothes, and you would know by the look on his face that he never expected to see the wheelwright.

"You came," says he, "for your son!"

"I did," says the wheelwright.

The Man in the Black Clothes clapped his hands and down flew a flock of pigeons and perched in the yard.

"You son is there, now," says the Man in the Black Clothes, "see if you can pick him out!"

And the wheelwright going from pigeon to pigeon said, "It isn't you anyway, or it isn't you, nor you …" till he came to this pigeon and he saw a crooked feather in his tail "Ah ha," he said "you're the one!"

"I don't know how you knew him," says the Man in the Black Clothes, very vexed, "so I'll let him go free on one condition. He can fly home as he is and if he can manage to wash his feet before I catch him your son is yours for evermore."

The pigeon flew away and the Man in the Black Clothes called his eleven sub-magicians and they changed themselves into twelve ferocious hawks and flew after him. And the pigeon looking back out of the corner of his eye saw the twelve hawks behind him, and he flew for all he was worth in the direction of home. 'Twas a long journey and looking back again he saw that the twelve hawks were coming nearer and nearer. Oh Glory! any minute now they'd pounce on him. The pigeon looked down and he saw the landlord's house below him, so to avoid the hawks he flew down the chimney and fell out into the room where the landlord's daughter was.

"Oh dear," says she, "the poor little pigeon all covered in soot!"

And turning, the nearest thing to her hand was the little golden basin and putting it under the tap she cleaned his feathers. And then she washed his feet in the golden basin and the pigeon changed into the wheelwright's son. It was many years since she saw him. But she remembered him and she remembered the dream. In time the wheelwright's son married the landlord's daughter, and in time too he fell in for all the property, and when he did he gave the poor people what they were always fighting for, and that was fair rent, fixity of tenure, and free sale, and what more could they want so they all lived happy ever after.

Bodach an Chóta Lachtna

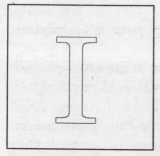t happened one day that Fionn and the Fianna were camped down on Beann Eadair and looking out over the ocean they saw approaching a ship in full sail, decked out in every colour and with gold and silver ornaments tacked on to the side of it.

When the ship drew in to the shore the sails were hauled down, and a big door opened at the side of it. The Fianna expected to see a huge army come marching out, but great indeed was their surprise when only one man came out and walked up towards them. And there is no man in Ireland to-day as good looking as he was, or no man as tall as he was for his head would touch the rafter.

He had on him a suit of armour studded with diamonds, on his head a shining helmet, in his right hand a long and treacherous looking spear, hanging from his left side a doubled edged sword, and over his shoulder a shield that showed the dint of many a battle. His name was Caol an Iarainn the son of the King of Teasáil* and he had come to conquer Ireland.

He walked up until he was face to face with Fionn the High King of the Fianna. Then Fionn spoke and said:

"We know what's on your mind, but before we begin to fight would you like to show your powers at some peaceful activity like racing or weight-lifting?"

"If there is any man in the Fianna," says the son of the King of Teasáil, "who'll challenge me to a race and if he wins that race I'll go home to Greece and do no damage here."

"Well now," says Fionn, "Caoilte Mac Rónáin the champion runner of the Fianna is not here to-day, he is below in Connaught, but I'll go down for him and while I'm away take off your coat of mail and make yourself at home with the Fianna."

So Fionn set out for Connaught and on the way he came to a dark wood with a wide road cut through the middle of it, and on this road

* Thessaly, in Greece

he saw approaching him a huge cumbersome figure—a great big ugly laughing clown, with a long grey top coat down to his heels. He had two legs under him like the two masts of a ship, and his shoes were like two rowing boats, and with every pace he took he splashed a barrelful of mud all round him, and the tail of his coat was so caked in mud that as he ran, it struck against the backs of his legs making a loud report that could be heard a mile away.

"Hoh, Hoh, hah, hah," he roared, "Fionn without the Fianna! Fionn going down to Connaught for Caoilte Mac Rónáin to race the son of the King of Teasáil," says he going into convulsions, "a man that'd pass out an express! Sure there's no one in Ireland could race the son of the King of Teasáil!"

"No one?" says Fionn.

"No one," says he, "but me!"

"You!" says Fionn, "'tis giving you enough to do to carry yourself with the weight of your shoes and the weight of your coat."

"Take me," says the stranger getting serious, "or you'll be the sorry man to-morrow."

"Alright," says Fionn, "and what is your name?"

"My name," says he, "is Bodach an Chóta

Lachtna."

The two of 'em turned back to Beann Eadair and when the Fianna saw Bodach and Chóta Lachtna and the size of him and the shape of him and the outlandish get-up of him it gave them enough to do to keep in the laughing.

"Is *he* the object I'm going to race?" says the son of the King of Teasáil.

"He is," says Fionn, "and what length do you want this race to be?"

"Three times three score miles," says the son of the King of Teasáil.

"Well," says Bodach an Chóta Lachtna, "it is that exact mileage from Beann Eadair in Co. Dublin, where we are, to Sliabh Luachra in Co. Kerry. We'll walk the track down to-night so that you'll know every twist and turn of it coming back tomorrow."

They set out, the son of the King of Teasáil and Bodach and Chóta Lachtna, and when they landed in Sliabh Luachra in Kerry, Bodach an Chóta Lachtna went to the wood and cut down timber and made a house, and he went to the wood and cut down timber and made a fire, and he went to the wood and killed a wild boar and with one clout of a cleaver he split the wild boar from the top of his snout to the tip of his tail, and put half of him turning on a spit in front of the fire.

Then he ran off to the barony of Inchiquin in Co. Clare and brought back a table and two chairs and two barrels of wine. When he arrived again in Kerry the side of the wild boar was cooked so he went to the door and called the son of the King of Teasáil into his supper. But he demurred saying he was of royal blood he couldn't sit at the same table as a harum-scarum like the Bodach.

"In that case," says the Bodach, "'twas idle for me to be bringing a second chair all the ways from the Co. Clare!"

So he sat down and finished one side of the wild boar and washed it down with a barrel off wine. He went out then and cut rushes, brought them in and made a bed and went to sleep for himself.

At the crack of dawn the son of the King of Teasáil woke the Bodach and the Bodach was furious saying he hadn't enough slept yet.

"But what about the race?"

"Be going away," says the Bodach, "and I'll get up to you."

He went off and the Bodach went back to bed for another hour. He woke then and cooked the second side of the wild boar and when it was done he ate it and washed it down with the second barrel of wine. Then he collected up the bones and put 'em all round inside the lining of his coat, and set out in the race picking a bone as he went and when the bone was bare throwing it back over his shoulder.

When he was a third of the way up through Ireland he passed out the son of the King of Teasáil and he kept on until he came to a tree loaded down with crab apples and he fell into munching the apples and after a time the son the King of Teasáil came up and he said to Bodach an Chóta Lachtna, "Your old top coat is torn to ribbons and there are pieces and tatters of it hanging out of every bush from here down to Co. Limerick!"

"Is that so!" says Bodach an Chóta Lachtna.

And he ran all the way back to Limerick picking the pieces and tatters as he went and when he had them all collected he sat down, took out a needle and thread and sewed them into the coat until it was as good as it was before and that would not be saying a great lot for it.

He set out in the race then and he was going so fast now that he passed out the wind in front of him and the wind behind him could not catch up to him. Two thirds of the way up through Ireland he flew past the son of the King of Teasáil. He kept on and when he was within five miles of Beann Eadair he came to a place where there were ripe blackberries, and as he was hungry again he sat down and ate his fill and when he was full he took off his long grey top coat and sewed it down the middle and made a sack of it. He filled the sack with blackberries and ran for Beann Eadair. And the Fianna seeing him coming far off said as sure as anything this is the son of the King of Teasáil having killed Bodach an Chóta Lachtna on the way and he was bringing him up on his back.

But when he came nearer they saw who they had and they ran to meet Bodach an Chóta Lachtna. But the Bodach was in no humour for conversation. "I'm hungry," says he. And he called for five sacks of flour and five churns of sour milk. And he kneaded the dough and made an enormous cake and he made a hole in the middle of the cake and emptied the sack of blackberries into it. He was building a fire then to bake the cake when who should the Fianna see coming but the son of the King of Teasáil and he was furious at being made a fool of before the world by this great, big, ugly, laughing clown, that he put

his hand on his sword ready for fight, but
before he had time to draw his sword Bodach
an Chóta Lachtna took up the cake of dough
and threw it with such force that it struck the
son of the King of Teasáil on the side of the
face and turned his head from back to front.
Then Bodach an Chóta Lachtna took him by
the hand and ran him down the side of the Hill
of Howth, threw him into the ship and shut
the doors and spinning the ship right around
he gave it one mighty kick that sent it seven
leagues out in the ocean!

So I'd say we'll hardly be hearing from the
son of the King of Teasáil for a long time to
come!

The Giant from Scotland

early everyone heard at
some time or other of
those grand people that
were living in Ireland long ago. I refer of
course to the Fianna, Fianna Eireann that
proud band of warriors that were there in
Fionn Mac Cumhail's time.

They were tall, graceful and comely, fleet of
foot, strong of arm, true to their word and
brave in battle. They lived their lives in the
open air hunting the deer and the wild boar,
playing hurling, putting the shot and all
forms of athletics. As well as that they were
trained soldiers, every one of them expert
with their sword, for they had to be always in
readiness to drive off whatever invader would
come to our shores.

There was great trouble in the world that
time too. Wars and rumours of wars, and

giants came from Greece to fight the Fianna, but if they did they were quiet men going home.

Now, at that time there was living in Scotland the biggest man that was ever in this world, and his name was An Fear Rua.* And one day didn't the notion rise in his head to hit for Ireland and challenge Fionn Mac Cumhail to a fight. So what did he do? What you'd expect. He pulled an ash tree out of the ground and lopping off the roots and the branches he made a walking cane for himself! That'll give some indication as to his size.

He set out and he kept going till he came to the sea and as he wasn't able to swim he lifted up big rocks, every one of them the size of a cathedral, and flung them into the ocean. These acted as stepping stones and as merry as you like he walked across and when he landed in Co. Antrim the place shook under the weight of him, ní nach ionadh!#

When the people saw him they were peppering with fright, but one man had the presence of mind to saddle his horse and gallop down to Co. Kildare to warn the Fianna that the Giant from Scotland was

* The Red Man.
# and no wonder!

coming and to be prepared.

Now, what happened that day but Fionn and all his warriors were out hunting. There was no one at home only the woman and Conán Maol. Conán Maol was a big, fat, lazy lump of a man without a single rib of hair between him and heaven, and a fresh round face like a full moon. He was a strong man afraid of nothing creeping or walking, but he'd be no match for the Giant from Scotland.

Fionn Mac Cumhail's wife, Gráinne, was a very clever woman, bright as a bee; there wasn't a wink over her, and like all women before and since she didn't want any fighting. So she hit on a plan that would send the Giant from Scotland trotting home in a bigger hurry than he came.

She made two cakes of bread and into the middle of one of 'em she put the griddle iron, and when they were baked she put them to cool on the window sill. Then she got all the women together and between them they sawed a number of planks into boards and made an enormous cradle complete with hood and rockers. Then they took the screens off the windows and they made a dress, like a baby's dress, for Conán Maol, and put it on him and a little flouncy cap, and one woman

took off her apron and tied it around his neck.
A dribbler by mar eadh!* Oh he looked
comical!

They put Conan into the cradle and began
to rock him, singing "Seo leo a thoil 's ná goil
go fóill."# Only that he was too heavy, I
suppose they'd be bouncing him up and down
and singing:

Throw him up and up
Throw him up in the sky,
Throw him up and up
And he'll come down by'n by.

With that they heard the cups rattling on
the dresser and the ground shaking under
them. The Giant from Scotland was
approaching and when he came into the yard
he called to Fionn Mac Cumhail to come out
and fight. All the women were for bolting the
door and let him bellow away outside, but
Gráinne, brave enough, went out and said
that her husband and the Fianna were gone
off hunting down towards Munster and she
didn't know when they'd be home.

The Giant said he didn't care if they didn't
come home for a year and a day that he'd
wait for them.

*   by the way.
#   "Sleep well my love, don't cry at all."

"And when they come," says he, "they'll meet their match in the Fear Rua."

"In that case," says Gráinne. "You might as well come into the house and sit down for yourself."

"Is it light in the head you are, woman," says he. "How could a man of my size go in through that small door!"

"Can't you do what my husband does," says Gráinne, "can't you lift up the house, walk in, and when you are inside let it down again."

He never thought of that. So he lifted up the house, and it gave him enough to do, walked in and when he was inside he let it down again.

"You must be hungry," says Grainne, "after your long journey from Scotland. There's a cake of bread for you. Make a mouth organ of it."

Well, with the first bite he bit the griddle iron that was inside in the cake—that was the one she gave him.

"Oh," says he, "my jaw is broken. This food is so hard that it would crack the teeth of a rhinoceros."

"Aren't you the delicate man by me," says she. "Sure that's the food we give the children. There's another cake on the window sill," says she to the women, "and give it to the child in the cradle and see will he object to it."

The other cake was given to Conán, and 'twas he made short work of it, a thing that surprised the Giant and no wonder for he thought there was an iron plate inside in that one too, and he said he'd give all the world to get one look at the little baby that could thrive on such a hard diet.

He was taken down to where Conán was, and when he saw the size of the "child" in the cradle his eyes widened in wonder.

"God bless the child," says he when he found his tongue. "I suppose he'll be soon walking. Has he all his teeth?"

"Everyone of 'em," they said. "Didn't you see him devouring the cake."

The Giant didn't believe this and what did the foolah do only put his finger into Conán's mouth.

"Oh," says he.

And only for he pulling it out so quick he'd be going home without it. Then he said in his own mind.

"If the children in Ireland are this size blessed hour tonight, what must their fathers be like!"

So lifting up the house he walked out from under it, and put it down again.

"It isn't going you are," says Gráinne.

"Oh I am," says he, "and I must hurry too or the tide'll be over the stepping stones."

And he walked off and he must have told all his brothers what happened for from that day to this no giant ever visited Ireland.

A bhuí sin do Ghráinne agus des na mnaibh eile. Sin é mo scéal sa.*

* Thanks to Grainne and the other women. That's my story.

The Wig and the Wag

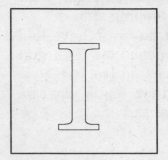

It wasn't in your time and it wasn't in my time, it wasn't in my father's time or in my father's father's time, it was away back in old Bett's time before the animals lost the power of speech and it is said to have happened in Co. Clare.

There was this woman and she was an odd woman and she had a small patch of black boggy ground, and she had half of it under potatoes for herself and the fowl, for she had an amount of them, hens, turkeys, ducks and geese, and the other half under grazing for the goat and the donkey.

She was a lone woman that always kept to herself, never making free with the neighbours and she lived in a small thatched house with one door, one window and one chimney. Very well why. She'd go twice a day

with the cliabh* to the cróitín# and she'd
gather up the eggs and put them in the big
ciseán⌀ by the dresser, a layer of eggs and a
shake of hay and the basket would be full by
Saturday.

Then she'd tackle the donkey and she'd go to
town and sell the eggs and buy the few
groceries for the week. It is little would do her,
living alone as she was in the house. And so
this went on till she was nearly as old as
myself and she wasn't able for the work
trifling and all as it was, so she let it be known
that she was on the look-out for a servant girl.

Droves of them came, for at that time the
country was teeming with people, and of all of
them that came there was only one she took a
liking to.

This girl was a long lanky one with a big
mothall** of red hair and she used to swagger
this way and that and she walking. Her name
was Juggy and the old woman hired her for a
half-a-crown and made known to her her
duties.

*   flat basket
\#   outhouse
⌀   basket
**   bushy head of hair

Juggy was to feed the fowl twice a day with pounded potatoes and a good shake of the fine Indian meal that was going at the time. She was to go with the flat basket to the outhouse every morning and every evening and gather up the eggs and put them in the big basket near the dresser. A layer of eggs and a basket of hay and the basket would be full by Saturday. She was to hang down three pots of water everyday, one to boil the potatoes for the fowl, one to boil the potatoes for herself and the old woman, and one was to wash their feet before they'd go to bed. She was to keep the kitchen nice and tidy, the floor swept and the delph shining. And in case the fairies would pay a visit during the night before she'd retire Juggy was to arrange the chairs around by the wall, everything in its own place, for the old woman said if she didn't do this she might find her left shoe above in the loft in the morning and the soap in the saucepan!

The old woman had great regard for the fairies, and for all we know maybe she was in league with them. All this Juggy was to do but there was one thing she was not to do and that was never to look up the chimney.

Juggy did as she was bid, observed all the rules and turned out to be a fine servant you may be sure. And everything went like clockwork till one Saturday when the old woman was in town, and whatever tempted Juggy didn't she look up the chimney! And what did she see above but a long leather bag. She pulled it down and ripped the cord that was tying the mouth of it, and 'twas full of shining sovereigns.

"Ah ha," says Juggy, when she saw the gold. "Why should I be killing myself here for a half-a-crown a week, when there is enough money here to keep me in comfort for a lifetime."

And putting the bag on her back away she walked wagging from side to side and shaking her head with the big bushy head of hair. And she kept going till she came to the banks of the Shannon. There she saw a boatman and showing him a gold piece she said:

"I'll give you that if you'll row me across the river to the boundary between the counties of Kerry and Limerick."

"Sit in," he said.

And he rowed her over to the other side and left her there digging with her hands in the sand.

Well now, it should be time for the old woman to be home from town. She landed and when she came into the yard she called:

"Juggy, come out and untackle the donkey."

There was no answer. She went into the kitchen and she called. "Juggy, Juggy, Juggy!" No answer. She came then to the door and shading her eyes she looked down toward Pairc na bPoll and Pairc a' tSasanaigh.* She looked in the high field and she looked in the low field but there was no sign of Juggy. Then she looked up the chimney and there was no sign of the leather bag!

Oh she was fit to the tied! And putting her hand on top of the dresser she took down her baitín draíochta#—'twas something like my walking cane—and away with her after Juggy and the first one she met was a little grey donkey with a short butt of tail busy keeping the flies off himself, so the old woman said to him.

"Did you see this girl of mine with the wig with the wag with the long leather bag that stole all the money I ever had!"

"Oh I saw her going down there a short time ago," the donkey brayed.

"She's livelier on the footing than I am," says the old woman, "and maybe you'd help me to catch up with her."

---

* The Field of the Holes and the Englishman's field
\# magic wand

"Hop up on my back," says the donkey.

And away he galloped, but as we all know donkeys are flaming rogues, so after a while he threw himself down on the road and would not move another peg. So the old woman was on her feet a second time. She walked on till she met a white pony and a red mare and she said to them:

"Did ye see this girl of mine, with the wig with the wag with the long leather bag that stole all the money I ever had!"

"With the wig with the wag?" they both said "with the long leather bag! She went down there a while ago."

"She's livelier in the footing than I am," says the old woman, "and maybe ye'd help me catch up with her."

"Hop up on my back," says the red mare.

"I can't," says the old woman, "you're too tall for me."

So the white pony put down his head and the old woman sat up on his neck holding on to his mane, and like a crane loading a ship he lifted her up and landed her on the red mare. And off they flew till they came to a swamp where the mare went down bogging and the old woman was on her feet a third time. She walked on till she came to where there was a meitheal* of men cutting the turf and she said:

"Did ye see that girl of mine with the wig with the wag with the long leather bag that stole all the money I ever had."

"We did," they said, "she went down there a while ago. Did she take much from you?"

"Cleared me out," says the old woman. "If I died tomorrow I couldn't rise to the habit! Maybe ye'd help me catch up to her."

"We will," they said. "And it is a good drumming she'd want when we catch up to her."

They kept running till they came to the banks of the Shannon where they saw the boat-man and he rowed 'em across the river, and they began to dig where they saw the fresh rooting in the sand, but there was nothing there. They moved up then on the high ground and who should they see going the coach road only Juggy with her wig with the wag but she had no leather bag!

The old woman called after her to know where did she hide the bag of money, but Juggy wouldn't tell.

"Alright so," says the old woman, "it'll be a long time until you get the good of it."

* a work party

And striking her baitín draiochta* three times on the ground, a h-aon, a dó, a trí,# she turned Juggy into a milestone until the year 2,000. Féach ar sin!ø—she'll be there for another eleven years!

So if there's anyone here that'll be going the way to Limerick in the year 2,000 let him keep a sharp look-out on the left hand side of the road and who knows but maybe he'll see Juggy with the wig with the wag with the long leather bag that stole all the money the hag ever had!

Sin críoch lem' scéal don babhta seo.**

---

*   magic wand
#   one, two, three
ø   Look at that!
** And that's the end of this story.

The Cat and the Splinter

t is only when you'd see the big blaze of electric light that's beaming down on me at the present moment, that you'd wonder how the people that came before use managed with the candle! or the rush light, or the splinter, for these were the only forms of illumination that were in the world before the oil lamp was invented.

At that time people living in the country made their own candles by getting a thin piece of cloth and twisting it and rolling it in melted fat—goat's fat, sheep's fat, or cow's fat. The fat was allowed to harden, and then the operation was repeated until such time as the candle was of the required thickness. The piece of cloth in the middle acted as a wick, and it gave fairish light.

Now, the rush light. This was an ordinary

rush you'd see growing in the fields. It was peeled so as to lay bare the white core. Well it wasn't peeled fully, a thin strip was left on for reinforcing. Then the rush was dipped in fat too, and allowed to dry and it gave a nice whitish flame, though to my mind it was not a permanent light, but it was handy if you were searching for something around the house or for showing the children their way to bed.

And this brings me to the third form of light—the splinter, which was made from bog pine, or bog 'dale' as we call it. When turf is cut away in the bog you'll often find down seven or eight feet trunks of trees lying at the bottom, and they're there for thousands or maybe millions of years, showing that there were great forests in Ireland one time. And I suppose these trees were knocked the year of the flood, and the bog formed over them. The timber in these trunks is as good as new for we all know that the bog has the effect of preserving anything that's hidden in it.

In the bad times poor people used bog 'dale' to roof the house and to make all the furniture that went into it. They had to, for they were not allowed by the landlords to cut the trees that were growing in the woods and they were too poor to go to the sawmills. But to come back to the splinter and how'twas made. You'd get one of these logs of wood that was taken out of the bog—a piece with a fairly straight grain—and you'd cut it into lengths of about ... say eighteen inches. Then you'd come with the hatchet and cleave them down, and split them into thin strips and put them seasoning for the winter.

That's a bog dale splinter. When the splinter was lit I suppose you'd have to hold it in your hand or put it into a crock on the table. I did hear it said that the women used to hold it between their toes, so as to be able to see while they were knitting. I think too that in nearly every house there was a bracket or a holder made by the smith driven into the wall, and when night would come a blazing splinter would be put in the bracket, and you had plenty of light then for playing cards or any other fun that would be going on. And how long would a splinter hold? Twenty minutes maybe, but when it burned out you could light another one, or two of them ... they were plentiful and there was no danger of blowing a fuse!

But to continue with my story. In the time of the splinters there was this carpenter and he was living alone. Well, I'm wrong, he wasn't entirely alone, there was a marmalade coloured cat in the house with him. The cat's name was Bubble, for he was big and he was fat and he was puffed out like a football. The carpenter was a first class tradesman, served his time, did journey work and he was in great demand in the locality for making farm carts and wheels.

In the kitchen he had his workshop, and in the winter time he used to work at night, making a wheel or maybe putting the body of a cart together on the floor. Fitting the laths between the shafts, putting on the left side-lace and the right side-lace, and the front set-lock and the back set-lock. The only light he had was the splinter, and he'd want it where he was working at the cart, and he'd want it at the table where he was cutting and planing, and he'd want it at the grinding stone where he was edging his chisels and as the man had only two hands he couldn't very well do his work and hold the splinter at the same time. So what did he do? He trained the cat that was known as Bubble to hold the splinter and to follow him around with the light. And if all belonging to you were dead you'd be in stitches if you saw Bubble holding the lighting splinter between his paws, and holding it out at arm's length so as not to scorch his whiskers. And here the carpenter used to be talking to the cat.

"Over this way now, Bubble. Over this way. Ah, no, no, no! To your left. Up more now, up! That's too high. Down a bit. That's it. Over now a small little bit to your right. Slant it a little bit more. Hold it there now, that's the tack. Good man, Bubble!"

And so this went on till the cat got so well up, that he'd know the carpenter's next move and he'd be there before him—if that cat was trained in time I'd say he'd be nearly able to make a cart himself and a pair of wheels. And this was miraculous, of course, and it wasn't long until the news got out about the cat holding the lighting splinter for the carpenter.

The cobbler told the saddler and the saddler told the smith. The thatcher told the cooper and the cooper thought he'd split, so he told the publican and the publican told the master and the master told the pupils, and the pupils told their mothers—and now everyone knew it. And before night fell the road was black with people all facing for the carpenter's house. You couldn't draw a leg in the yard, and there they were jostling and swaying and craning their necks and standing on their tippy-toes trying to look in the window. And when they saw the cat they said:

"Will you look at him! Isn't he a pure marvel. If he was mine I wouldn't part with him for a bane of cows."

Now, it so happened at that time that there was a travelling showman going around the country with performing fleas, cockroaches and all kinds of small animals. He had them in boxes and if you gave him a penny he would let you see this menagerie doing tricks. He came one night to the carpenter's house. The carpenter was having his supper at the time and when the showman saw Bubble sitting on his corrigiob* in the middle of the table, supporting the blazing splinter, he was speechless, for he couldn't believe that such a thing was possible. When he found his tongue he said to the carpenter:

"How do you account for this?"

"Training," says he, "training, it defeats nature."

"I don't believe a word of it," says the showman, "of all the animals in this earth the cat is the hardest to teach and the quickest to forget his training."

* haunches

"I'll bet you anything you like," says the carpenter, "that this cat won't forget his training."

"Alright," says the showman, "we'll soon see!"

And what did he do? He put his hand into a box and let a mouse go on the table, and like lightning the cat dropped the splinter and left the two of them in the dark! Is treise an dúchas ná oiliúint agus sin é mo scéal-sa dhíbh anois.*

* Nature beats training. My story is told.

The Small Red Bull

here was a rich man living in Ireland long ago and he had a small red bull. Oh, a very valuable animal and he wouldn't part with him for love or money. The man was married and all the family he had was an only son, and the son's name was Liam.

When Liam was very young his mother died, but before she was called away she made her husband promise that he'd give the small red bull to Liam. The husband said he would, and he was true to his promise and he gave the small red bull to Liam to keep him always.

Now it so happened that the man married secondly and the woman he married had three daughters of her own and these were called Cucadú, Cucadaoí and Cucadáró—strange names and strange people too, wherever they came from, for the step-mother had no love for

Liam. She wanted him out of the way so that the property would fall to her own daughters Cucadú, Cucadaoí and Cucadáró. So every morning she used to send Liam herding cattle to the hill and she would not give him any breakfast going, any dinner to take with him, or any supper when he came home in the evening.

But strange as it may seem Liam was never hungry and he had all the appearance of being well fed. And where was he getting the food? That was the mystery. The stepmother said she'd find out, and one fine morning she sent her eldest daughter Cucadú with Liam herding the cattle to the hill. She told Cucadú to keep her eyes open and to see what was happening.

They went to the hill Liam and Cucadú and when the sun was high in the heavens Liam said: "I suppose it is time we had our dinner." And he picked a leaf of sorrel that was growing near him and he began to chew it. He picked another leaf and gave it to Cucadú and she began to chew it and if she did she fell asleep. When she was asleep Liam called "Hó i leith! Hó i leith! Hó i leith!"* and up came the small

* "Over here! Over here! Over here!"

red bull and taking one of the horns off his head, he struck it on the ground. And lo and behold out of the horn came a lovely little house, and in the house there was a chair and a table and on the table every kind of food and drink you could wish for. Liam sat down on the chair and ate his fill and when he had enough to eat the house and the chair and the table disappeared into the horn and the small red bull put the horn on his head and walked away down the field grazing with the cattle.

Cucadú woke up by 'n' by not one whit the wiser, and when they went home in the evening she told her mother that all Liam had for his dinner was a leaf of sorrel.

"A likely story," says her mother, "I'll send Cucadaoí to keep an eye on him tomorrow."

She did and when the sun was high in the heavens Liam said: "I suppose it is shoving near dinner time."

And picking a leaf of sorrel he began to chew it, and picking another leaf he gave it to Cucadaoí and she began to chew it and of course she fell asleep. When she was sound asleep Liam called, "Over here! Over here! Over here!" And the small red bull came up and taking one of his horns from his head he struck it on the ground and there was the little house and the chair and the table and Liam sat down to a feast fit for a king, and when he had enough to eat the house and the chair and the table and the crockery disappeared into the horn and the small red bull put the horn back on his head and walked off down the field grazing with the cattle.

In a while's time Cucadaoí woke ignorant of what took place and when they went home that evening she told her mother that all Liam had for his dinner was a leaf of sorrel—duilleog amháin a' tsamhaidh.* So the third daughter Cucadáró said she'd go herding the cattle with Liam to the hill tomorrow. She went and when the sun was high in the heavens Liam said:

"I suppose it is time hardworking people were sitting down to their dinner."

And he took a leaf of sorrel and began to chew it and he handed another leaf to Cucadáró, but Cucadáró cute enough wouldn't take it.

"I've bread and milk here," says she, "which I brought them from the house in the morning and it will do me fine." Wasn't she clever!

And, of course, when she didn't chew the leaf

* only one leaf of sorrel

of sorrel she didn't go to sleep. The day wore on and the small red bull was wondering why Liam wasn't calling "Over here! Over here! Over here!" and he said to himself, "Isn't it a long time poor Liam is going without his dinner," and finally about four o'clock in the evening he ran up to where Liam was sitting and taking one of his horns from his head he struck it on the ground, and wasn't that the surprise Cucadáró got when she saw the little house and the chair and the table laden down with every variety of food and drink—you wouldn't see the likes at a wedding! Liam sat down on the chair and ate his fill and when he had enough the little house and all the furniture disappeared into the horn and the small red bull put the horn back on his head and walked away down the field grazing with the rest of the cattle.

When Cucadáró found her tongue, she said, "Ah-ha-dee! Wait till my mother hears about this," and she ran home and told her mother. Seodh, when her mother heard the story she didn't say "yes, "aye" or "no" only took to the bed and let on to be dying, mar eadh.* And when her husband came in in the evening he

* by the way.

said to Cucadú, Cucadaoí and Cucadáró: "Where's herself?" "She's in bed," they said. "What's wrong with her" says he. "She's dying!" they said.

Up with him to the bedside and he said to his wife, "Will I bring you the doctor"

" 'Tis no use," she said.

"There's only one thing will cure me now. You must kill the small red bull and make beef tea for me."

The husband was very down and out when he heard that and he said wouldn't any other animal do to kill to make beef tea. "No," she said, "only the small red bull."

"Alright so," he said, "I'll kill him tomorrow." And he went and he told Liam and Liam didn't close an eye that night and at the crack of dawn in the morning he ran to the hill and told the small red bull what was going to happen.

"Why then," says the small red bull, "I won't be here when they come for me. I'll run away and if you take my advice you'll run away too for what's my turn to-day might be your turn tomorrow. Hop on my back and we'll go away for ever."

Liam hopped up on his back and they galloped away like the wind and never drew rein until late that evening they came to a house and that house was the King's palace.

"Go up now," says the small red bull, "and knock at the door and if the King asks what brought you say 'I came to marry your daughter'."

Up with Liam and knocked at the door and the King came out and said:

"What brought you?"

And Liam said, "I came to marry your daughter."

"Well now," says the King, "I'll ring a bell at eight o'clock tomorrow morning and you must go and hide somewhere and if my soldiers can't find you before I ring the bell again at four o'clock in the evening then we can talk, only talk mind you, about marrying my daughter. Have you me?"

"I have," says Liam, " 'Tis a very hard task but I'll chance it."

The King brought Liam in and gave him his supper and after the supper there was singing and dancing until it was eight time to go to bed. And when the bell rang at eight o'clock in the morning Liam went out and spoke to the small red bull.

"Tell me," says Liam, "where do you think would be a good place for me to go in hide?"

"Well now" says the small red bull, "as luck would have it a rib of hair fell out of my tail this morning, and let you go in where the hair fell out and it will be the clever detective that'll find you there."

A thing that was true for him. Liam went in where the hair fell out and he had plenty of room there. The King and his soldiers began searching, and they searched high up and low down in field, haggard and orchard; there wasn't a nook, hole corner or cranny that they didn't look into, and of course they failed to find him and when the bell rang at four o'clock Liam hopped out and went into the palace.

"Well now" says he to the King, "you'll have to give me your daughter in marriage."

So Liam married the King's daughter and he lived happy from that day out and the small red bull was always there to advise him, and he forgot all about the hard life he had living in the same house as Cucadú, Cucadaoí and Cucadáró.

The Golden Steed

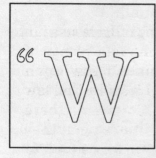

"When the roses bloom
again down by the
river,
And robin redbreast sings his heart's
refrain,
For the sake of old langsyne I'll be with you
sweetheart mine
I'll be with you when the roses bloom again."

There was a King in Ireland one time and another King in England, and when they were young they were in the same school together in France. There was a very up-to-date academy there at that time for training kings.

Well, it seems they became great friends, so much so that when their schooling days were over they used to visit each other during the holidays every year. As time went on they got older and they got married, and when their fathers died they had to take over the throne and the crown, and they were so taken up now running their own affairs of their two countries that a great number of years went by without their meeting at all.

Well, one fine day the King of Ireland said to himself:

" 'Tis a long time now since I saw my old friend over in London. I'd know in the world how is he getting on."

He drew down this to his wife and his daughter, an only daughter is all he had, and they said that now as everything was done, the hay in, the turf ricked and the oats threshed, wouldn't it be a right good notion to take on a trip to London to see the King. The women of course were mad for the road! He agreed, so they got ready for the journey and set out.

Now, as luck'd have it, around the exact same time the King of England said to himself:

" 'Tis a long time now since I saw my old friend over in Ireland. I'd know in the world how is he getting on!"

He drew down this to his wife and his son, an only son is all he had, and they said as everything was done now, peace in the world an a few more countries conquered, wouldn't it be a right good notion to take on a trip to Ireland to see the King. He agreed and they packed their cases, got ready for the journey and set out.

And of course what happened was when the King of Ireland got into London he heard there that the King of England had come to Ireland. And when the King of England got into Dublin he heard there that the King of Ireland had gone to England! 'Twas all very comical. And both sides were kicking themselves that they didn't send word beforehand to say they were coming, but the way it was they wanted to have it as a surprise.

Well there was nothing for them to do now only go away home again, which they did. And the two ships that were carrying the two parties met in the middle of the Irish Sea. They drew up, and they all went on board one ship, and they laughed enough at what happened.

The two Kings had a lot to talk about and it was decided then and there, that they'd remain on board one ship and sail away on a sight-seeing tour for the space of a week. And the result of this was that the King of England's son and the King of Ireland's daughter became very friendly. She was a lovely girl. Marriage was mentioned. Well, the fathers and mothers were delighted at this, and they gave their consent and arranged that the wedding would take place when the King of Ireland's daughter would be twenty-one years of age. That would be in three years time.

They all went home then and the young couple were looking forward to the big day. Ah, but look at the strange turn things can take. What happened the following year but the King of Ireland to get killed in some battle, and in the cuff-huffling that went on after, it wasn't the King's daughter was put on the throne at all but a fly-by-night of an uncle she had, and of course he made new laws and regulations and one of the things he knocked on the head was her proposed marriage to the son of the King of England.

He said that the King's daughter should marry a man of his own choosing. He had it all planned, and he brought this man, a neighbouring chieftain, to the palace. Oh an ugly looking gazebo, and when he put the question "Will you marry me?" to the King's daughter, she didn't refuse him outright, for she knew it would be no good for her. But she hit on a plan to keep putting the wedding on the long finger till she'd be twenty-one years of age. So she said:

"I won't marry you until you bring me a dress made of green rushes."

He went and he brought it and he said:

"Will you marry me now?"

"I won't marry you now either," says she "until you bring me a dress made of shining shillings."

He went away and he brought it to the King's daughter and said:

"Will you marry me now?"

"I won't marry you either," says she "until you bring me a dress made from all the coloured feathers of all the birds in the air."

He went away and he was a long time gone getting a feather here and getting a feather there till he had one belonging to every bird. The job she gave him.

Then he had the feathers made into a dress and he brought it to her and said:

"Will you marry me now?"

"I will," says she, "but first I'd like to see the wedding present you're going to give me."

"What would you like?" says he. He hadn't even thought of a wedding present. "What I'd like," says she, "is a horse made of gold."

Now this was a job that couldn't be done in a day, or in two days or in a hundred and two days. He went away, and it wasn't a blacksmith or a silversmith he gave the job to but to a goldsmith. Then one night the king's daughter made off to the goldsmith and she said:

"Whatever money that chieftain is giving you to do the work, I'll give you as much more if you can put a secret door on the side of the horse with a lock on the inside of it."

He said that it would be a knacky work, but that he'd do it. He did, and when the horse was ready 'twas brought to the palace and the wedding was to take place on the following morning. The very day, by the same token, the King's daughter would be twenty-one years of age.

She didn't go to bed at all that night only remained up baking, and putting her belongings together, and at the dead of night, when everyone was in blanket street she took her belongings and the bread and went into the inside of the horse and locked the door. She hadn't much room, the poor thing, and only for the goldsmith leaving the horse's mouth open she'd stifle inside!

In the morning all those that were invited to

the wedding were arriving, and when the time
came for the ceremony to begin the Chieftain
looked around and there was no sign of the
King's daughter. They searched high up and
low down but she was nowhere to be found.
Then her uncle and the Chieftain and
everyone there saddled their horses and went
off looking for her.

When they were gone, who sailed into the
bay but he King of England's son, and himself
and his warriors came up the palace to find no
one there but the girl's mother. She told the
King's son all that happened. He was very
down and out when he heard it. The girl's
mother told him too how loyal her daughter
was to him. How she kept putting off her
marriage to the Chieftain from day to day by
asking him for a dress made of green rushes, a
dress made of shining shillings and a dress
made of coloured feathers, "and the last thing
she asked for," says she, "was a horse made of
gold an there 'tis there standing beside you."

"And isn't it a lovely ornament" says he, "a
Golden Steed." Of course he didn't know no
more than a crow what was inside in it.

"I'd like," says he, "to take it away as a
keepsake."

"You're quite welcome to it," says she.

So he got his warriors to load the horse of gold on board the ship, and he took it away over to London, and erected it on a platform in front of the palace. The following day he was outside in the front lawn drilling his soldiers—left, right, left right, left right— when the door at the side of the horse opened and the King of Ireland's daughter put her head out and said "Halt." Well the start that was knocked out of the King's son! But when he saw who he had he was delighted, and the two of them were married before the week was out, and everyone that was anyone was at the wedding, and the song the King's son sang was:

"When the roses bloom again down by the river,
And robin redbreast sings his heart's refrain
For the sake of Old Langsyne I'll be with you sweetheart mine
I'll be with you when the roses bloom again."

A Bright May Morning

ay Day is the first day of Summer, and long ago in Ireland there were many customs and piseógs too, connected with May day, Lá Bealtainne.

In a good many places before the sun would rise on May morning, the people used to go out to the wood and bring in branches of greenery, hazel and holly and elder and rowan, and they'd come dancing through the fields, chanting:

Samhradh, samhradh, bainne na ngamhna,
Thugamair féin an samhradh linn.
Thugamair linn é, is cé bhainfeadh dinn é,
'S thugamair féin an Samhradh linn.*

* Summer, summer, milk for the calves,
  We brought the summer with us.
  We brought it with us and who'd take it from us,
  We brought the summer with us.

They'd bring the green branches into the house, hanging a big one maybe on the outside of the door. Then, when the rising sun'd light up the yard and shine into the kitchen they'd greet the summer saying:

"Come, sit you down on a chair of silver!
Come, sit you down on a chair of gold!
You are welcome my brother to linger here
    with us,
'Tis long since we saw you and we're tired of
    the cold!"

The winters were very severe at that time. But it was grand to be young with the young Summer when the trees were out in all their finery, and the fields were decked with flowers. And you'd see young calves with white faces dancing in the leaca,* the cock strutting around the yard his comb as red as a coal of fire, hens clocking in the hayshed, dogs barking turning in the cows, and little yellow chickens poking their heads through their mother's wings to see what all the fuss was about.

And do you know a job we'd love when we were very small, to be sent out in the fields to pick wild flowers to decorate the May altar, for there was one in a prominent position in every

* sloping field

house at the time. There was to be sure!

But a lot of the old people believed in the fairies too, and they considered it very unlucky to give away a coal of fire on May Day. And they believed that a neighbour if he was bad enough, could take the "profit" of a farmer's produce and leave him poor for the rest of the year. And you'd hear it given down that there were witches there in those far off times who could change themselves into the shape of any animal.

Very well why. There was this man and his name was Jeremiah, and he went out one May morning to turn in his cows to be milked. He had two dogs and they ran on before him and he heard them barking in the fields as if they were giving chase, and fearing that they'd upset the cows he put his fingers in his mouth and whistled. The dogs came back but they were very agitated and wild to be off again. But he said, "heel up! heel up there!" and being well trained they remained at his heels.

He brought home the cows and he and his wife Jude milked the cows and put the milk in wide shallow pans on the stellan.* When the cream rose to the top of the milk Jude skimmed off the cream and put it in the cream

---

* Stand to hold milk pans.

tub. Many is the small lad raided that tub, but he was always caught. The white moustache would give him away! When the churning day came around Jude put the cream in the churn, but if she was pounding it with the dash till Ireland was free from shore to shore the cream wouldn't crack. In other words it wouldn't turn into butter. They had nothing to sell at the market, there was little or no money coming into the house and they were badly off.

And to add to their misfortune a very valuable horse they had strayed.

Jeremiah tried the neighbourhood, made enquiries at the school and the master asked the scholars but no one saw Jeremiah's horse. Jeremiah went to the May fair and at that time there was a bellman in town and for a small fee he'd publish whatever it was you wanted him to publish.

Jeremiah gave him the description of the horse and one and sixpence and the bellman went off through the fair ringing his bell and proclaiming:

Ting-a-ling-a-ling-a-ling-a ling. "Strayed from the property of Jeremiah P. Hanniffin a five year old bay cob with white markings on his forehead and fetlocks. Anyone having information about this valuable animal should send word to Jeremiah P. Hanniffin of Gortamuchlach." Ting-a-ling-a-ling-a-ling.

But strange to say no one came forward with information as to the whereabouts of the five year old bay cob.

Jeremiah came home very disappointed to his wife, and the following day he set out to tramp the roads of the barony making inquiries at every house. He was away all that day and all the following day and the third day coming up to dinner time he saw a house back from the road and he said to a man passing:

"Who is living there? They might know something about my horse that's missing."

And the man said:

"No one around here goes near that house, for the old woman that's living there is an unwholesome person. She trucks in magic, and do you know what I'm going to tell you, she's a witch!"

"If she is any good at that trade," says Jeremiah, "maybe she could tell me where my horse is."

He went up and knocked at the door and there inside he saw this terrible old woman.

"What are you looking for," says she.

"My horse that strayed from me," says Jeremiah.

"Let me close my eyes," says she, "until I see all the fields in the world. Now describe your horse to me."

Jeremiah described him.

"Breá bog, she said. "Ná h-abair focal anois. Bí ciúin, bí ciúin, bí ciúin!"* Ah ha, I see him. Grazing in Pairc na gCloch in the townland of Cillínluachra. Hurry up or he might be gone."

Jeremiah was out the door like a shot and he made a bee line for Pairc na gCloch and there sure enough was the horse. Jeremiah was delighted and he brought him home. But he was still without the profit of his milk so he said: "I'll be up before day next May morning to see who is tampering with my cows!" And he was up before dawn that day, and he hid himself where he had a good view of the macha\# where the cows were. He had his two dogs with him and the horse saddled. Dawn broke and the heavens brightened, but he could see no one coming to the fields. The sun would soon be rising and he was about to come out of his hiding place when he saw a hare hop in over the ditch. He took no notice of that, but when the hare sat under a cow and began to

* "Fine and easy," she said. "Don't say a word now. Be quiet, be quiet! Be quiet!"
\# Name given to field where cows are kept at night

milk her he got the surprise of his life and when the hare went from cow to cow doing the same thing, he let go the dogs and said, "Go on, sketch him! Hullahull, hullahull!"

Off went the dogs after the hare, and Jeremiah jumped on the saddle horse and the chase was on. I tell you that hare could travel, and many was the turn he knocked out of the dogs, darting this way and darting that way, up hills and down hollows, into fields, over ditches and dikes, along high ground, low ground, hard ground, wet ground, rocky ground and sometimes they were going at such speed they didn't know what kind of ground was under them, till they came to a part of the country Jeremiah thought he had been in before. There in front of him he saw a certain house, and the hare made for it, and rounding the ditch of the yard one of the dogs bit the hare in the leg. Well, the hare let out a screech, and when Jeremiah rode up he was nowhere to be seen but the dogs were scraping down the door. Jeremiah opened the door and went in and there he saw the same old woman and she breathless like she'd be after running and her leg all cut. "Ah ha," says Jeremiah to her, "you are found out!"

"Save my life," says she, "I won't do any

more harm to you or any one else, I'll never run like a hare again. I'm crippled after that dog."

"Alright," says Jeremiah, "if you promise to give over your capers."

She said she would and he came home and thanks to be goodness he had no more trouble making the churn. Jude had plenty of butter to sell in the market and enough money to do them, and herself and Jeremiah lived happy from that out.

The Cat and the Yard of Cloth

here was this man and he was a rich man, and he was living in Ireland a long time ago.

Three sons is all the family he had and their names were Cormac and Manus and Malachy. When their father died he left his mansion, and a fine mansion it was, to Cormac; he left his land and a fine lot of land he had, to Manus, and all he left to Malachy was a cat and a yard of cloth.

Malachy was very down and out when he heard this, but the cat spoke up and said:

"Things could be worse. Fold the yard of cloth in two, get a needle and thread and sew it up the two sides and make a bag and the two of us'll go away and seek our fortune."

Malachy folded the yard of cloth in two, got a needle and thread and sewed it up the two sides and made it into a bag, and himself and the cat set out to seek their fortune. They walked on all that day and when night came they went into a wood and lay down under a big tree on a bed of leaves, and soon they were in slumberland.

At the crack of dawn the following morning the cat got up and taking the bag he went to the hill and killed a rabbit, and putting it in the bag he set out and never drew rein till he came to the King's palace, and going up he knocked at the door. A servant came out and the cat said:

"Could I see the King?"

"Hold on there awhile," says the servant.

He nearly dropped with fright when he heard the cat talking, and he went in and he said to the King.

"There's a cat outside at the front door and he says he wants to see you."

"That's funny," says the King, "a cat wanting to see me! Hah, hah, hah. Wonders will never cease. Tell him to come in."

The servant came out and he said:

"He'll see you all right. Come on away in." "Very good," says the cat. "Am I presentable?"

"Well now," says the servant, "you'd want to wash your face then."

So the cat licked his paw and washed his face, and the servant brought him a looking glass and the cat looked into it and preening himself he said:

"Ah here, I suppose I'll do."

And off with him into the palace and opening the bag he took out the rabbit and said to the King.

"That's a present from young Malachy, a man there wasn't much heard of up to now but there will be before long."

And without giving the King time to open his mouth the cat turned on his tail and ran out the door and came back to the wood. The following morning the cat went deep into the forest and killed a cock pheasant. He put the pheasant into the bag and set out and never drew rein till he came to the King's palace and going up he knocked at the door. The servant brought him in and the cat, opening the bag and taking out the cock pheasant, said to the King:

"That's a present for you from young Malachy, a man there wasn't much heard of up to now but there will be before long."

"You don't say!" says the King

"I do say," says the cat.

Turning on his heel he left the King there

the height he grew. The cat came home and the following morning he went fishing, and whatever bait he was using it must be the right one for he caught a fine salmon and putting the salmon in the bag he set out and never drew rein till he came to the palace and said to the King.

"That's another fine present from young Malachy, a man there wasn't much heard of up to now but there will be before long."

And then the cat sat down on his corrigiob* and looked up at the King and said:

"Have you any message for young, Malachy?"

"I have," says the King. "Tell him I want to see him here at the palace tomorrow at twelve o'clock. I've a job for him."

"Tá go maith,"# says the cat, "I'll tell him what you said."

The cat came back to Malachy and that night when they were about to lay down on the bed of leaves under the big tree in the wood the cat said to Malachy:

"In case I'd forget ... and I knew I had something to say to you ... the King is expecting you at the palace tomorrow at

* haunches
# "Good,"

twelve o'clock. He has a job for you."

"Are you in earnest," says Malachy.

"How could I appear before the King in these old clothes, and I've no money to buy a new suit."

"You needn't worry about clothes," says the cat.

In the morning the two set out and when there were a half a mile from the palace they came to the river and when they were crossing the footbridge the cat put out his leg and tripped Malachy and he fell into he river and got all wet.

"Maith mar a tharla,"* says the cat running up and telling the King that Malachy fell in the river.

"He is all wet!" the cat said.

The King gave him a new suit of clothes and when Malachy put this on he was so respectable that you could take him anywhere. They went up to the palace and when they came to the gate the cat said:

"I'll wait here now till you come out."

Malachy was inside a long time and when he came out he said to the cat.

"That's a nice thing you walked me into. The

---

* It is well how it happened

job I got! I'll have to go off now and kill a giant
that's terrifying everyone in this territory.
And not alone is he a giant but he's a magician
as well. He's called the Gruagach na gCleas*
and anyone that ever went after him never
came home alive. You're the sore cat to me,
yourself and your capers."

"And supposing you do succeed in killing
him," says the cat.

"Well if I do," says Malachy, "I'm at liberty
to marry the king's daughter and I'll fall in for
the whole kingdom when he retires himself."

"Isn't that something to look forward to,"
says the cat. "Come on and we'll kill the
giant."

They set out and when they came to the
giant's mansion the cat said to Malachy:

"You wait here now and watch us in through
the window and I'll go in and have a talk with
himself."

The cat knocked at the door and the giant
said:

"Shove it in, 'tis open."

The cat opened the door and said:

"Ah, ha, you think you're smart."

"I am smart," said the giant, "and I know it."

* the tricky or wily magician

"Could you do this so?" says the cat.

And balancing himself on his two front paws he walked around the floor, and the giant stood on his hands and walked after him. Then the cat turned himself into a cartwheel and bowled around and the giant did the same and bowled after him.

"Show me that ring you have on your finger," says the cat.

The giant took off the ring and the cat turned himself into a mouse and ran in and out through the ring. Then reverting to his natural shape he said:

"I'll bet now you couldn't do that."

"What a lot of bother that'd be to me," says the giant, turning himself into a mouse. And if he did the cat put down his paw and killed him.

They took the giant's ring back and showed it to the King, what more proof did he want, and Malachy married the King's daughter and himself or the cat never saw a poor day from that out.

The Changeling

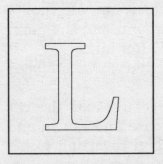ong ago in Ireland if people saw a very beautiful young woman they would say to her parents:

"Guard her well or the fairies might steal her and leave a changeling in her place!"

And the fairies who lived under the raths and forts of Ireland at that time were believed to do that very thing, if they wanted a bride for a fairy man, who was too old to get a young wife among his own people. And this is one of the stories I heard about a fairy changeling.

There was this couple living in a place called Rockfield, and all the family they had was one son and the son's name was Timmie. They had no land much, and Timmie's father used to work for his day's hire for a rich farmer during the Spring and Summer months. He wouldn't venture out at all from October to March for as he said the wet didn't suit him, and it didn't for he was a delicate sort of person.

When Timmie was a nice hardy youth he used to go every day with his father to the rich farmer's house, and the farmer used to give him odd jobs to do like stowing on the cows, calling the men into their dinner and looking after small animals—calves, lambs, goslings an bonavs. Timmie loved his work and it gave him a feeling of importance to be allowed sit at the same table as the workmen every day for his dinner and he'd get a few shillings every week going home to his mother.

Now in that same house there was a small daughter and her name was Kate. She was around the same age as Timmie, so that they grew up together and they were great friends. By the time Timmie was a young man he was able to turn his hand to any sort of work on the farm, but he was only getting the same few shillings going home every week. He thought he was worth more, and this evening he approached the farmer looking for a rise in pay as he was doing a man's work now. The farmer said he couldn't see his way to give it to him. They had words, and the farmer said if you don't like what you are getting here you can go elsewhere. Timmie said he would and he went away.

Now when the workmen came into their supper that night young Kate and her mother wanted to know where Timmie was. "I'll tell you after," says the farmer. Cute enough he didn't want to say what happened in case the workmen would want a rise in pay too.

But when they went home Kate and her mother said:

"Well, where's Timmie?"

"Ah, he was looking for a rise in wages," says the farmer, "and I couldn't see my way to giving it to him. We had words and he went away."

Kate was very sad when she heard that and her mother said:

" 'Twas a bad right for you then to let him go, for no nicer youngster ever came inside the door of this house. I was as fond of him as if he was my own son. To let him go for the sake of a few shillings! I'm very upset about it and Kate is very upset too." And Kate was!

"Well if that's the way ye feel," says the farmer, "I'll go down to the house in the morning and tell him to come back."

He went down to the house in the morning only to meet by Timmie's mother and she very down and out, the poor woman, for Timmie didn't come home at all the night before.

What happened you see was Timmie was so upset over the row he had with the farmer that he walked away across the country. He didn't know where he was going and late the following day he was passing through Ardanaonaig, and enquired from a man he met if he could direct him towards Bailemhúirne. Whatever put it into his head to go there.

"Right," says the man, "go up Glenflesk over the Bounds and down the The Mills and you're there."

Timmie went off and between calling into one place for his dinner and into another place for a drink of milk he was delayed. You wouldn't miss the time going talking. The night overtook him on the road and he went astray in the dark and wound up going around in circles in Crócháin Wood behind Loobridge.

Out in the night the moon showed a little, but Timmie was so tired he said he would stretch down on the withered leaves and wait for daylight.

He wasn't long there when he heard all the clitter of talk coming towards him—"call wup a gcupaldee, backadash bee"—and he couldn't make out a word they were saying. And who would be out at this hour of the night in such a lonesome place. He ducked in behind a tree not wishing to become involved, and along they came passing within a hand's reach of him and who was there but the Coill Chrócháin fairies. In the light of the moon he could see them as plain as I see my finger, and they were of all shapes and sizes, small, bearded, little cabaires,* long lanky scúrlúns# and big bulky bromaires∮ with faces as ugly as a bulge in a broken bucket, but in the middle of them all there was one very handsome face he thought he knew very well.

Timmie said he'd follow on to see what was going to happen, and on the way, to be on the safe side, he took off his coat and turned it inside out. A very wise precaution. The procession came to an opening between two rocks and went in Timmie at their heels and they came to a high round room and a tree growing in the middle of the room. There was a big crowd there and a man in a blue coat playing music on the comb.

A door opened at the sides and the doorman

* gabby fellows
# long-necked
∮ fat-bottomed

said "Bígí in úr dtost!"* And out walked the Cathaoirleach# and sat down and said "Is everything set for the wedding?" And the crowd shouted "Everything right!"

"Very well" says the Cathaoirleach# "Send out the bridegroom!"

The bridegroom came out and without one word of exaggeration his beard was so long that they had to put a knot in it to keep him from walking on it. The Cathaoirleach# shook hands with the bridegroom and said:

"Cad is ainm duit?"ø

And the bridegroom said: "Eamon is ainm dom."**

"And when were you born?"

"The night before the Battle of Benburb!"

"Your realise the importance of this undertaking," says the Cathaoirleach.#

"I'm long enough thinking about it," says he.

"My sound man" says the Cathaoirleach,# "send out the bride."

'Twas then the ree-raw and cuffhuffling began and over it all a young girl was heard shouting, "Are ye out of ye'r minds! I wouldn't

* Be silent
# Chairman
ø What is your name?
** My name is Eamon

marry him if he was the King of Bulgaria!" And with that she was pushed through the door and up to where the Cathaoirleach* was sitting. And Timmie wouldn't believe his two eyes and his heart came up into his mouth with fright when he saw who was there. Who was it but Kate the rich farmer's daughter that was carried off that night by the fairies and an iarlais or what in English is called a changeling left in her place.

The Cathaoirleach* came to attention and said: "Anyone here having any objection as to why these two should not be man and wife?"

"Faith then," says Timmie, jumping to his feet, "you can put me down as having a big objection."

And making a road up through the crowd flattening the fairies at both sides of him he took Kate by the hand, and was she glad to see him!

"Come on," says Timmie, "and we'll hit for home."

"Play tough," says the bridegroom rolling up his beard and tucking it inside his waistcoat, "you won't take Kate out of here without a fight."

* Chairman

"Put up the dukes!" says Timmie.

And they squared out and old and all as the lad with the beard was you never saw such sparring, and the knacky footwork of the little caffler! Timmie kept drawing him till he got an opening and then he landed him with a palltóg* of a clout that lifted him fifty feet into the air and when he was falling the knot in his beard got entangled in a branch of a tree! There he was suspended and while the fairies were wondering whether they should call the fire brigade to bring him down Timmie and Kate ran out of the place like the sí ghaoithe#.

They hadn't long to wait for daylight and they went into the first house they saw where they met a knowledgeable woman. When she heard what happened she handed Timmie the "cochal bunach."Ø "Put that in your pocket," she said, "you'll want it when you go home." She called her son then to give Timmie the loan of the saddle horse and Timmie hopped into the saddle and lifted up Kate behind him and in no time at all they were in Rockfield.

Timmie told Kate to wait there near the hayshed, and he went into the farmer's house

---

* thump
# fairy wind
Ø little hemp bag

and the kitchen was full of relations all very mournful and Timmie, not letting on a bit, said, "Where's Kate?"

"Is that the way 'tis with you," they said, "she's in the throes of a fever and not expected to do the day!"

Timmie went up to the room and there was the rich farmer and his wife bemoaning the fact that what they thought was their daughter was soon to die, and you couldn't blame them for being fooled for the changeling in the bed was the exact image of Kate.

"'Twas nice of you to come," says the farmer's wife, "but I'm afraid there's no hope for poor Kate."

"Ah I wouldn't give in to that," says Timmie taking the "cochal bunach"* out of his pocket and whatever power was in it, when the fairy in the bed saw it she let a screech out of her, and went into a spin like a gig and went out through the roof. Timmie told them then what happened and he went out and called in Kate and the farmer and his wife couldn't thank him enough and as they had no son of their own he got the farm and he married Kate, and you'll see their grandchildren in town any day you'll go to a football match.

* little hemp bag

The Wolf and the White Kid

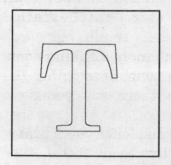

There was this little grey nanny goat in the world one time and she was known as the Gabhairín Riach, and she was living in a tiny house by the edge of a big wood. She had no family, we're told, except one small kid, and oh! she was daft out about him, for he was young and he was playful and he was giddy and he was pure white and the name she called him was Báiní.

This day, and a fine summer's day it was, the nanny goat said to the small white kid:

"Now Báiní," says she, "to-day I'm taking a canter into the wood."

"And will you bring home something for me," says Báiní.

"I will to be sure," says she, "I'll bring home some nice greens, and then the two of us can sit down and have them for our supper. Won't that be lovely!"

"But what will you bring me," says Báiní.

"I'll bring you," says she, counting 'em out on her fingers. "Bileóga a' spoinnc, bileóga a' t'Samhaidh, bláth an taithéalain, caisearbháin cos-dearg, deas ruadh, agus seó rudaí mar so dom mhaicín beag féin, dom leanaibín gleóite. Báinín beag, deas óg!"

"Now," says she, "what are you going to say!"

"I'm going to say," says he, "that you'll bring me leaves of coltsfoot, leaves of sorrel, the flower of the wild woodbine, the red legged dandelion and a holy show of other nice things for your own little son, your own lovely, young, little Báiní! Isn't that what you said?"

"That's what I said," says she, "and when I'm gone I implore of you to close the door and bolt it. In these troublesome times you'd never know who'd come and carry off poor Báiní. Don't open the door for anyone now, not even for the King of England. And when I'll come home, I'll call you. You'll know your mother's voice, but to make double sure I'll put my foot in under the door, and when you'll see my foot you'll know it is your mother that's there, and then you can draw back the bolt and open the door for me. What did I say now?"

He told her what she said word for word and
then the Gabhairín Riach went away and
when she was gone Báiní shut the door and
bolted it.

Now, who should be outside hidden behind
a sally tree but a wolf, and when he saw the
nanny goat going into the wood he said to
himself.

"Ha, ha, ha. Now is my chance to go into the
goat's house and carry off that kid and he'll
make a fine supper for me to-night."

Up to the door with him and he tried it and
greatly to his dismay he found that it was
locked. So what did he do only change his voice
so as to sound like the nanny goat and he said:

"Open the door a stór.* Open the door and let
me in."

"Who is outside?" says Báiní. "Who is calling
me?"

"Who is calling you," says the wolf, "but your
mother. Open the door and let me in."

Báiní remembered what his mother told
him so he said:

"Put your foot in under the door until I see
it."

The wolf put his paw in under the door.

"Eyeyeh," says Báiní when he saw the paw.

* my treasure

"What in the world is this! Go away," says he, "clear off with yourself. You are not my mother whoever you are."

When the wolf heard that he put on his thinking cap, and he closed his eyes and he said:

"I'll have to work the head to get the upperhand of that kid."

When he opened his eyes what should he see but a little donkey foal that had strayed away from his mother. The wolf ran down and marched the donkey foal up the goat's house warning him on the way not to open his mouth or make any noise, and then the wolf altering his voice as before so as to sound like the nanny goat said:

"Open the door a stór.* Open the door and let me in."

"Who's outside?" says Báiní. "Who is calling me?"

"Is it the way you don't know your own mother," says the wolf. "Open the door, son."

"Put in your foot so," says Báiní, "until I see it."

The wolf nudged the donkey foal and whispering out of the side of his mouth he said:

* my treasure

"Go on, put in your foot or I'll give you a welt."

The foal did and when Báiní saw the tiny little hoof appearing under the door he was nearly taken in by it, but on closer examination he saw that there was no cleft on it, so he said.

"Clear off. Go on. Make tracks. You are not my mother. You are only trying to take a rise out of me."

The wolf turned away and said to himself:

"Why then if the cat went a pound as sure as your name is Báiní I'll get you out of that place."

He sauntered down the field and what should he see but a young deer, a fawn, and he marched him up to the goat's house and when Báiní wanted to know who was outside—

"Your mother," the wolf said.

And when Báiní said, "Put your foot in under the door so until I see it."

The wolf nudged the deer and told him to put his foot in under the door, and when Báiní saw the respectable little hoof he was full sure and certain it was his mother's and what did he do only draw back the bolt and opened the door. And God help us tonight the creature, that was the fright he got when the wolf rushed in, caught a hold of Báiní and walked away with him no one knows where.

And when the nanny goat came home from the wood with all the nice things for the supper and when she saw the door of her house wide open, and when she looked in and saw that Báiní was gone she went clear out of her wits—pure distracted and she ran here and she ran there calling his name and saying:

"Where are you Báiní? Báiní! Báiní! Báiní!" But it was all to no avail there was no answer. And she thought then that maybe it was the fox that came, for he is a hanging rogue ... ho! ho! well we know it. So she ran to the fox's house and the fox was pure indignant that she should think of such a thing and he swore by this and by that, the sop and the rock and the comb of the cock and the depth of the well ... "if I ever," says he, "laid as much as a finger on your son Báiní."

The nanny goat then thought that maybe it was the wild cat. You had these in Ireland long ago, and ferocious boyos they were. And she ran out to the wild cat's house. The wild cat spat fire and fury and said:

"That I may be laid as low as Nell the Tub or hung as high as Gilderoy if I ever as much as clapped an eye on your son, Báiní."

Who would she go to now and she thought of the black raven and she went, and he had good news for her. And wasn't it grand to hear it! And he said:

"I was up in the air a while ago looking down and seeing everything that was happening below, and I saw the wolf carrying off Báiní, and he put him in the cave at the foot of the hill and blocked up the opening. Then he went away saying to himself and I heard what he said and these are his very words:

"I'm not hungry enough yet," says he, "for my supper, so I'll take a saunter for myself in the fresh air to get an appetite."

"Then he walked away up to Carrigín na Gréine and putting his two paws behind his head he stretched out sunning himself delighted with his day's work and looking forward to his supper."

The Gabhairín Riach didn't wait to hear any more only ran to the foot of the hill and tore down whatever was blocking the opening of the cave, and there inside she saw Báiní.

"Come on," say she, "and we'll run home."

"Oh we will," says Báiní, "we'll run as hard as ever we can."

And as they were running home who came overhead but the raven very excited and he said:

"Do you know who's coming up the valley now? A man with a gun, and I'll go an tell him where the wolf is on Carrigín na Gréine and that wolf'll get what's coming to him."

"Oh do," says the nanny goat.

"Oh do," says Báiní.

And they ran home and just as they were sitting down to their supper they heard a shot.

"What was that?" says Báiní.

"That," says his mother, "is the end of the story. The wolf is as dead as a door nail and we needn't be afraid anymore."

So the Gabhairín Riach and Báiní the white kid lived happy from that day out.

The Fairy Twins

nnsan atán sibh arís. Dé bhur mbeatha. Well, bhfuil aon scéal agaibh dom. Muna bhfuil, tá scéal agam díb.

Long, long ago, if you wanted to have a new suit of clothes made you'd go to the draper's shop and buy a suit length ... so many yards of cloth ... we'll say now three and a half yards would make a suit for me. As well as the suit length you'd have to get what was known as the trimmings. They were lining for the inside of the coat, material for the pockets, buttons of course, big and small, padding for the shoulders of the coat, stiffening for the collar, a couple of reels of thread and backing for the waistcoat.

Well, these were all put in a paper parcel and you'd bring the parcel home and wait for one of the travelling tailors that used to be going around the country at the time to call the way. He'd live in the house until such time as the suit was made. He'd have a bed every night and he'd have his breakfast and his dinner and his supper every day. And there he'd be working away sitting cross-legged up on the table cutting and stitching and sewing an ironing and talking and laughing for these tailors were a very airy crowd.

Now, the first thing he'd do was take your measure and then cut the cloth according to your size, going to great trouble with the coat—I'm told there's no trade at all in making a trousers, I could nearly make one myself! But the coat is tricky to get it perfect, and if it isn't made right it might be up at the collar, or maybe it wouldn't close, or it might close in such a way that there would be room for two people inside in it. Wouldn't that look smart! But if the tailor knew his job the suit would be such a perfect fit that you'd look like as if you were spilled into it.

But to returned to the travelling tailors. The man I knew when his day's work would be over he could turn his hand to anything in the line of entertainment. He could sing, dance, play the fiddle, solve riddles, do tricks or tell a story. And many is the story he had about the fairies. I can tell you, you would not be lonesome with him. And I remember one night my mother saying to the tailor:

"I suppose there's no truth in this rumour that the fairies will take a good looking baby out of the cradle and put an ugly one in his place."

"Oh indeed," says he, "you can be sure there is, for I saw a case of it myself. Did ye ever hear," says he, "of a townland called Kippach." And we said we did.

"And did ye ever hear," says he, "of a family called Kissane that were living there."

"We did of course," we said, "why wouldn't we."

"In that case," says he, "throw another few sods of turf on the fire and draw up ye're chairs until I tell ye of an adventure I had."

So we heaped turf on the fire and pulled up in a circle around him. He put away the pipe he was smoking and throwing his eyes to the rafters he waited for silence. Then he said:

"For all the world 'twas in the month of May and I was at the market in Killarney one Saturday when I met a man called Kissane from the townland of Kippach. We were talking, Kissane and myself, and he took me of material for a Sunday suit he wanted for himself. He said his sister and her husband were coming home from America and he wanted to appear respectable before them.

Very well why, we went into Hilliard's, and as sure as I'm sitting here he fingered every single roll of cloth in the shop before he finally decided on a piece of blue serge material that was likely to wear well. Then after a further bout of haggling with the shopkeeper over the price, the suit length and the trimmings were papered up, and Kissane said to me.

"Come here, what day will you be coming over to Kippach to make the suit of clothes for me?"

"I'll be over to you Monday," says I, "without fail."

"Well now, that's awkward," says he, "I'll be away Monday in the bog cutting turf."

"What difference does that make," says I, "can't I take your measure now. Sure I won't want to see you again until we're ready for a fit on."

"Fine out," says he, "that suits me."

So I took out my tape and measured him from head to toe, and wrote down the particulars in my book, and he took his parcel and went away.

"Bhí go maith agus ní raibh go
h-olc."* Monday morning bright and early I
set out for Kippach, a long tiresome journey
over the mountain, and when I arrived there
Mrs Kissane was preparing to take the dinner
to the bog to her husband. She welcomed me,
got my own dinner ready and I sat down to it
for I was hungry. Sitting there and looking
around the kitchen I saw two cradles on the
flag of the fire.

"What's this?" says I.

"Twins," says she.

"God bless 'em," says I. "Aren't they
lovely"—and they were not you know!

"Are they gone off to sleep?"

"They are," says she. "And that's the only
time we have any peace in the house. They're
so cross and so peevish, and I wouldn't mind
but up to the time they were six months old
they were two lovely boys and so good looking.
Then one night they were alone here in the
house and when I came in after milking the
cows I noticed the change in them. They
aren't like my own children at all."

"Did they talk yet," says I.

---

* It was good and it wasn't bad.

"They didn't talk nor walk," says she, "or they have no notion of it. Make very little noise now and don't wake 'em while I'm out."

She went away and I began to work, when after a while I thought I heard a conversation coming from the cradles. I cocked my ear. And one of the twins sat up in the cradle and said.

"Bhfuil sí féin imithigthe amach. Is herself gone out?"

"Oh she is," says the other twin.

"She's gone with the dinner to the bog to old Kissane."

They didn't see me at all, I kept as quiet as a mouse hiding under the table.

"Well, in that case," says the first twin, "we might as well provide ourselves with a little amusement to pass an idle hour."

And what did one twin do? Thunder and turf! I couldn't believe my eyes, he put his hand under the cloths and took out a fiddle. And putting the butt of it under his chin he drew the bow across it. He didn't like the sound it made, so he put away the bow and tightened up two of the strings. He tried again with the bow, and the sound must be to his liking this time, for he began to play, singing at the same time.

Take her away down to the quay,
I won't marry her at all to day.
She's too tall and I'm too small
I won't marry her at all, at all.

With that the other twin hopped out of the cradle and taking down a dinner plate from the dresser and putting it in the middle of the floor, he began to dance inside in the plate. Well, if you saw them!

"These are not natural children," says I to myself, trying to keep serious. Then I got a tickling in my nose Ah......ah tishoo! I sneezed. The two of them looked around and when they saw me there were livid with rage, and began pelting me with cups and saucers from the dresser. I had to protect myself so I put the tongs in the fire. One look at the hot iron was enough for them they ran out the door and I shouted after them saying:

"Take care now," says I. "That ye'll send back the two small babies that were stolen from this house."

When Kissane and his wife came home from the bog in the evening you could knock them down with a feather when they saw the two cradles empty.

"Oh Dia linn,"* says the woman, "where are

* O God be with us

my two small children gone?"

"They ran away," says I, "and you are well rid of them, the little fairies," telling her exactly what happened. "And my advice to you," says I, "is to put the cradles outside the door to-night."

She did, and when she went out in the morning there were her two children. The fairies put them back, and they were not one whit the worse for their experience, and they grew up to be two fine handsome men. And where are they now? One of them is married at home in Kippach, and the other is in New York, I saw a letter from him. He's down in the subway driving an electric train.

That is my story about the fairy twins directly as I heard it from an airy tailor long ago.

Children's
POOLBEG

Orla Was Six
  Mary Beckett £2.99
Candy on the Dart
  Ita Daly £2.99
*When the Luvenders
  Came to Merrick Town*
  June Considine £3.50
Discoveries
  Clodagh Corcoran ed £4.99
Baker's Dozen
  Clodagh Corcoran ed £3.50
Children's Quiz Book No. 1
  Robert Duffy £2.99
Children's Quiz Book No. 2
  Robert Duffy £2.99
Joe in the Middle
  Tony Hickey £2.99
Where is Joe?
  Tony Hickey £3.50
Spike and the Professor
  Tony Hickey £2.99
Blanketland
  Tony Hickey £2.99
The Bridge of Feathers
  Eamon Kelly £2.99
The Turf-Cutter's Donkey
  Patricia Lynch £2.99
*Brogeen Follows the
  Magic Tune*
  Patricia Lynch £2.99

*Brogeen and the Green
  Shoes*
  Patricia Lynch £3.50
Patsy-O
  Bryan MacMahon £2.99
Growing Things
  Sean McCann £2.99
*Shoes and Ships and
  Sealing-Wax*
  A Book of Quotations for Children
  Sean McMahon ed £2.99
*The Poolbeg Book of
  Children's Verse*
  Sean McMahon ed £4.95
The Viking Princess
  Michael Mullen £2.99
The Little Drummer Boy
  Michael Mullen £2.99
The Little Black Hen
  Eileen O'Faoláin £2.99
An Nollaig Thiar
  Breandán Ó hEithir £2.99
Bugsy Goes to Limerick
  Carolyn Swift £2.99
Robbers on TV
  Carolyn Swift £2.99
A Little Man in England
  Shaun Traynor £2.99
Hugo O'Huge
  Shaun Traynor £2.99

The Turf Cutter's Donkey

and

Brogeen Follows the Magic Tune

by Patricia Lynch

"Classics of Irish Children's Literature"

Irish Independent

POOLBEG

The Poolbeg Book of
Children's Verse

Edited by Sean McMahon

A sparkling miscellany of poems for the
young and everybody else.

"Already a classic,"
RTE Guide

POOLBEG

Irish Sagas and Folk Tales

by Eileen O'Faoláin

Here is a classic collection of tales
from the folklore of Ireland

POOLBEG